ALL GOD'S CRITTERS GOT A PLACE IN THE CHOIR

ALL GOD'S CRITTERS GOT A PLACE IN THE CHOIR

words and music by
Bill Staines

pictures by Margot Zemach

E. P. DUTTON · NEW YORK

Words and Music copyright © 1978 by Mineral River Music
Illustrations copyright © 1989 by Margot Zemach

Published in the United States by
E. P. Dutton, New York, N.Y.,
a division of NAL Penguin Inc.

Published simultaneously in Canada by
Fitzhenry & Whiteside Limited, Toronto

Designer: Riki Levinson
ISBN: 0-525-44469-6
Printed in Hong Kong by South China Printing Co.
First Edition   10 9 8 7 6 5 4 3 2 1

for Karen, Bowen, and Hallie

B.S.

for my sister, Amielle

M.Z.

All God's critters got a place in the choir—
Some sing low, some sing higher,
Some sing out loud on the telephone wire,

And some just clap their hands

Or paws

Or anything they got. Now . . .

Listen to the bass, it's the one on the bottom

Where the bullfrog croaks and the hippopotamus

Moans and groans with a big t'do,

And the old cow just goes "Moo."

The dogs and the cats they take up the middle,

While the honeybee hums and the cricket fiddles.

The donkey brays and the pony neighs

And the old coyote howls.

All God's critters got a place in the choir—
Some sing low, some sing higher,
Some sing out loud on the telephone wire,
And some just clap their hands
    Or paws
        Or anything they got. Now . . .

Listen to the top where the little birds sing
On the melodies with the high notes ringing.
The hoot owl hollers over everything,
    And the jaybird disagrees.

Singing in the nighttime, singing in the day,

The little duck quacks, then he's on his way.

The possum ain't got much to say,

    And the porcupine talks to himself.

All God's critters got a place in the choir—
Some sing low, some sing higher,
Some sing out loud on the telephone wire,
And some just clap their hands

Or paws

Or anything they got. Now . . .

It's a simple song of living sung everywhere

By the ox and the fox and the grizzly bear,

The grumpy alligator and the hawk above,

The sly raccoon and the turtledove.

All God's critters got a place in the choir—
Some sing low, some sing higher,
Some sing out loud on the telephone wire,

And some just clap their hands

Or paws

Or anything they got NOW!

CHORUS

All God's crit-ters got a place in the choir—Some sing low,

some sing high-er, Some sing out loud on the tel-e-phone wire, And

some just clap their hands Or paws Or an-y-thing they got. Now...

VERSE

Lis-ten to the bass, it's the one on the bot-tom Where the

bull-frog croaks and the hip-po-pot-a-mus Moans and groans with a

big— t'-do, And the old cow just goes "Moo."

VERSE

The dogs and the cats they take up the mid-dle, While the

hon-ey-bee hums and the crick-et fid-dles. The don-key brays and the

po—-ny neighs And the old coy-o-te howls.

CHORUS

VERSE

Lis-ten to the top where the lit-tle birds sing On the

mel-o-dies with the high notes ring-ing. The hoot owl hol-lers o-ver

ev-er-y-thing, And the jay-bird dis-a - grees.

VERSE

Sing-ing in the night-time, sing-ing in the day, The

lit-tle duck quacks, then he's on his way.— The pos-sum ain't got much— to say, And the por-cu-pine talks to him-self.

CHORUS

VERSE

It's a sim-ple song of liv-ing sung ev-ery-where By the

ox and the fox and the griz-zly bear,_ The grum-py al-li-ga-tor and the

hawk a-bove, The sly rac-coon_ and the tur-tle-dove.

CHORUS

All God's crit-ters got a place in the choir—Some sing low,

some sing high-er, Some sing out loud on the tel-e-phone wire, And

some just clap their hands Or paws Or an-y-thing they got NOW!

DISCARDED